CRITTERS

BY R. A. NOONAN

Crestwood House
New York
Collier Macmillan Canada
Toronto
Maxwell Macmillan International Publishing Group
New York   Oxford   Singapore   Sydney

With thanks to
Chris Biggs, Steve Chiodo, and Gene Warren
for sharing their adventures
behind the scenes.

Macmillan Publishing Company
866 Third Avenue
New York, NY 10022

Collier Macmillan Canada, Inc.
1200 Eglinton Avenue East
Suite 200
Don Mills, Ontario M3C 3N1

Printed in the United States of America

First Edition

10 9 8 7 6 5 4 3 2 1

Noonan, R. A.
    Critters / by R. A. Noonan.—1st ed.
        p.   cm.—(Tales of terror)
    Summary: Pursued by bounty hunters from the prison asteroid from which they have escaped, alien creatures called crites land on Earth and start to eat all the living things they can find. A section at the end of the book reveals how the special effects were done in the film version of this story.
    ISBN 0-89686-575-4
    [1. Science fiction.] I. Title. II. Series.
PZ7.N753Cr 1991
[Fic]—dc20
                                                                90 45819
                                                                        CIP
                                                                        AC

Photography from the film *Critters* courtesy of New Line Cinema Corp. © 1990 New Line Cinema Corp. All rights reserved.

Cover and series design by R studio T.

DEEP IN SPACE . . .

A lone ship moved through deep, dark outer space. Up ahead loomed its next stop, an asteroid. The small, rocky planet was a space prison.

"Radio control, do we have permission to land?" the ship's captain asked.

"We've been expecting you," said the voice on the ship's speaker. "You're the ship carrying the ten crite prisoners, right?"

"We have only eight prisoners now," the captain explained. "The crites were eating everything in sight! We had to kill two of them to make the food last."

"Roger. You are cleared for landing," said the controller. "Put the prisoners in the security cell as soon as you land. And be careful. Those crites are dangerous!"

BREAKOUT!

Warden Zanti was worried. As warden, he was in charge of all the prisoners on the asteroid. And now something was wrong with the crites. Zanti floated down the hall. He had to get to the control panel.

Although Zanti had a human face and hands, he was not an earthling. Instead of walking on legs, he floated on a round disk. And Zanti's head was hairless and shiny and white.

Zanti rushed up to the controls. Red and blue lights flashed on the wall behind him. The alarms were going wild. Suddenly, a blast rocked the prison.

Zanti gripped the controls. "What's going on?" he shouted.

"There's been an explosion in the security cell," a voice reported.

"What about the crites?"

"They seem to be missing, sir."

A moment later, a frantic voice cut in. "This is the docking area. **3**

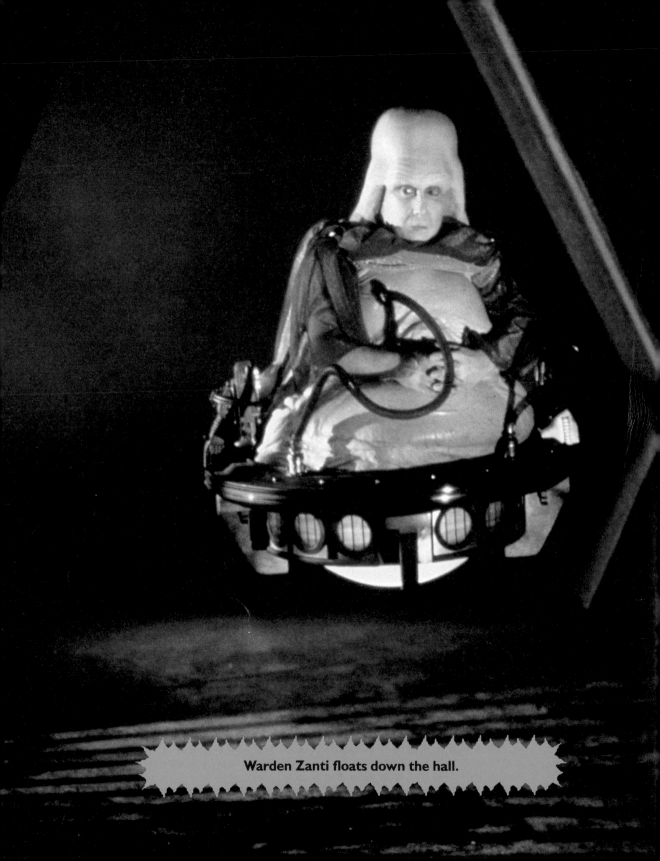

Warden Zanti floats down the hall.

They've stolen a ship," it said. "The crites are leaving the asteroid with one of our fastest ships!"

Creases formed on Zanti's forehead. He couldn't let the evil crites escape. "Fire on them!" he ordered. "We must stop them."

As the stolen ship lifted off, the prison guards fired on the crites. Deadly blue laser beams streaked through space. But the runaway ship dodged the fire.

Warden Zanti saw it all on the screen in the control room. The crites had gotten away. They were dangerous. He would have to track them down and destroy them.

"Get me the bounty hunters," he ordered.

THE HUNT BEGINS

The bounty hunters climbed into the seats of their spaceship. Without a word, they strapped themselves in.

Zanti floated between them. "I have a job for you," he said. He told them how the crites had gotten away.

"They seem to be headed for a far solar system," Zanti said. "The ship they stole has lots of fuel. But they will need food. Crites are always hungry. That's why we think they're headed for earth. There are millions of living things there. The crites will have a feast!"

The two hunters had the bodies of rugged men. But their faces were smooth, white masks. They were ready for the crites. Each hunter had strapped on a belt with a knife and a laser gun. And both hunters wore brown leather armor with steel studs.

"You must stop the crites before they feed," Zanti warned. "You should have no problem fitting in on earth. Just transform your faces."

The hunters were able to change their faces. By transforming, they could look like anything in the universe.

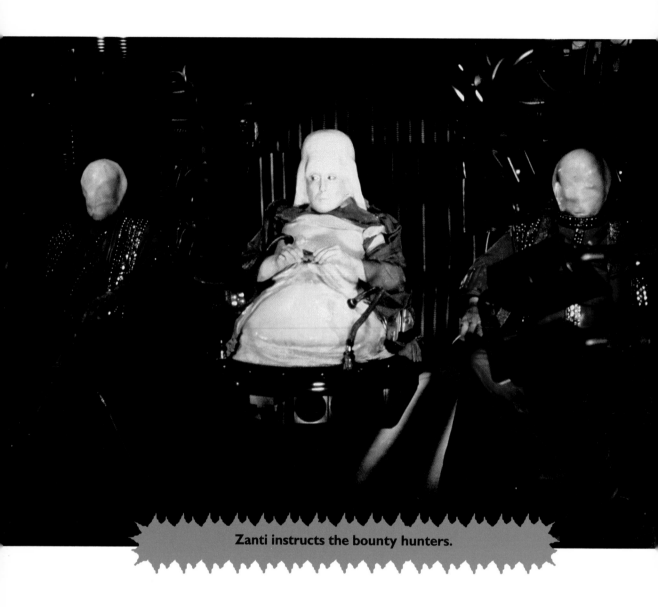

Zanti instructs the bounty hunters.

Before he left the hunters' ship, Zanti gave one more order. "Destroy the crites," he said. "But please don't make a mess of planet earth."

The hunters turned away. They hated being told how to do their jobs. Flipping switches, they prepared for takeoff.

 **LIGHT IN THE SKY**

Twelve-year-old Brad Brown was in trouble. His father had laid down the law. No supper. No movies for two weeks. And no more slingshot.

It was his sister's fault. From the window of his room, Brad could see his sister, April, and her boyfriend outside in the darkness. They were sneaking into the barn to listen to music. And he was stuck here.

Brad had been sent to his room for using his slingshot to zap April. But it wasn't his fault.

That afternoon, Charlie McFadden had been practicing with Brad's slingshot. Charlie had hit April by accident. But since Charlie could lose his job for goofing off, Brad had taken the blame.

Charlie helped Brad's father run the family farm in Kansas. The job was good for Charlie because no one else would hire him. People in town thought he was crazy. Charlie liked to tell stories. He told everyone that Martians talked to him through the fillings in his teeth.

Brad liked having Charlie around. He didn't mind sticking up for him. But Brad did mind that his teenage sister always got her way.

Brad's dad had taken away his slingshot. But he still had his homemade firecrackers. Brad scooped them up and stuffed them into his pockets. Maybe he could get back at his sister by setting off one in the barn.

Climbing out the window, Brad crawled across the roof. Then he reached up and swung into a nearby tree. He was just about to climb down when he saw it. A bright yellow ball bolted across the night sky.

"Wow!" Brad gasped. Then the ground began to shake. The tree rocked so much Brad almost fell.

Brad sees a fiery ball in the sky.

As soon as the rumbling stopped, Brad heard the screen door of the house slam. It was his father.

"You'll miss the bowling contest," Brad's mother called from inside. Brad's father had a special bowling match that night.

"I'll be right back," said Brad's father. He jogged down the path. He stopped when he saw Brad perched in the tree.

"What are you doing up there?" Jay Brown asked.

Brad had to think fast. He was supposed to be grounded. "The earthquake threw me clear out of my room!" Brad said. He could tell that his father didn't believe him, though.

"Get down here, son," Mr. Brown ordered.

Brad climbed down the tree. "Did you see that meteor?" he asked.

His dad nodded. "I saw something."

They headed down the path. "Maybe it's a Russian spy plane on a secret mission," Brad said.

His father sighed. "I think you watch too much TV."

THE FIRST ATTACK

In a nearby field, the spaceship was still smoking. Inside, eight crites cackled.

"What now?" one crite asked.

"Food!" the others shouted.

One by one, the crites rolled out of the ship. They looked like brown, furry softballs. The balls tumbled across a wheat field until they came to a grazing cow.

Suddenly they stopped rolling. They stood up. Their red eyes glowed. Their sharp, spiked teeth gleamed as they circled the cow. The attack was quick. They bit into the cow, tore its flesh apart, and munched.

It was feeding time.

The spaceship lands.

TRANSFORM!

The hunters' ship landed on earth. Inside, one hunter flipped a switch to turn on the video screen. Pictures of earth flashed on the screen.

The hunter found most of the information boring. But he liked the rock video of Johnny Steel. As the hunter watched the music video, his face began to transform. Sparks flew from his head. First he became an ugly skeleton. Then coarse, red muscles formed, and his face was sticky with blood. A minute later, milky white skin formed on his face.

When he was completely transformed, he looked just like Johnny Steel. He had Steel's long brown hair, gray eyes and wide mouth.

The hatch slid open. The hunters climbed out of the ship. They didn't have to walk far. In a nearby field they saw the mauled body of the cow. They could tell that the crites had made it to earth.

"Feeding has started," said one hunter.

The bounty hunters aboard their ship.

WILD ANIMALS

Brad heard the scream as soon as he walked in the door. It was his mom. He and his dad rushed into the kitchen.

Brad's mother stood in the center of the room. She was shaking and pointing at the window over the sink. Broken pieces of a plate were scattered on the floor. "Something was staring at me from outside," she said. "It had big red eyes."

Jay Brown went to the back door. He shined his flashlight over the trash cans behind the house. "I don't see anything," he said.

"Maybe it was Chewy," Brad said. Chewy, the Browns' cat, liked to climb on things. But Brad didn't really think his mother would be scared by the cat.

Brad bit his lip. Something was creeping around outside. It seemed to be a hungry critter too. Brad and his father had found a dead cow out in the back field. The cow had been torn apart and eaten alive. Brad had never seen anything so gross.

Brad's father picked up the phone. "The sheriff should know what's going on out here," he said. "Maybe he's gotten other calls. He can send Jeff out to look around." He finished dialing, then frowned. "That's strange." He tapped the phone. "The line is dead."

Suddenly, the lights flickered. Then they went off. The whole house was pitch black.

OUT OF CONTROL

Deputy Jeff Barnes was in a hurry. He had to change clothes at home, then drive back to town for the big bowling contest. He was driving too fast to stop when something furry dashed across the highway.

Jeff hit the brakes. The car skidded off the road.

"That darn dog!" Jeff exclaimed. When the dust cleared, he

looked up from the steering wheel. He was in a ditch beside an empty field.

The deputy got out of the car and searched the weeds and bushes. "Here, pooch," he called. He wanted to catch the stray dog. Otherwise, it could cause a bad accident. "Come on, doggy," said Jeff. He inched along beside the police car.

Suddenly, he felt a terrible pain in his leg.

Jeff fell to the ground. There was a thin, gray dart sticking out of his knee. What kind of animal could *shoot*?

Jeff heard a strange growl under the car. When he looked over, his heart started pounding. A critter was coming toward him. Its pointy teeth glimmered. Its red eyes glowed.

And the critter seemed to be smiling. The sharp teeth were the last thing Jeff saw before the hungry critter dragged him under the car.

Jeff is dragged under the car.

Brad's father searches the cellar.

DOWN IN THE CELLAR

Brad helped his father heave open the cellar door.

"It'll only take me a second to check the fuse box," said Jay Brown. "Wait here."

The cellar was very dark. Brad's father held up his flashlight. One look told him that someone had been here. The room was a mess. Tools littered the floor.

Brad's father peered at the fuse box. The wires were shredded, as if they had been chewed by an animal.

A low growl came from one of the shelves. Brad's father froze. So the animal was still here.

He could see a fuzzy ball on one shelf. Was that Chewy? He reached over to touch the fur, and the critter bit him.

"Aah!" Jay Brown staggered backward.

The critter attacked again. This time it jumped onto the man's shoulder. Its teeth sank into his flesh.

Brad's father wrestled with the critter. He tumbled against the wall and fell on a box. His hands ripped at the fur, trying to pry the thing off. But the monster's jaws were locked on his shoulder.

Finally, he tore the critter lose. Blood soaked his shoulder as he ran to the stairs. His feet slipped on the bottom step, and he stumbled forward.

The critter shot a needle-thin dart across the cellar. It stuck in Jay Brown's shoulder.

"Aah!" he screamed again, gripping the stairs.

"Dad!" Brad yelled. Seeing that his father was in trouble, he raced down the steps. With a tug, he pulled his father out of the cellar.

"What was that?" Brad asked as he slammed the cellar door.

"I don't know," said his father. "But it sure is mean and hungry."

Brad helped his father into the kitchen. Jay Brown was weak with pain. Brad's mother washed off his wounds. As Brad watched, his father pulled a thin dart from his shoulder.

"I can't feel that arm," said Brad's father. "There must be some kind of poison in that thing."

Brad picked up the dart. It looked like a needle or a thorn. It was only three inches long. How could such a small thing hurt his father so much?

Brad studies the poisonous dart.

B LOOD IN THE HAY

April's laughter filled the barn. She sat across from her boyfriend in the hayloft. Steven always knew some great jokes. He was telling her another one when the music stopped. The tape had ended.

"I'll get that," he said. Steven reached up to where the tape player sat on a bale of hay. His fingers were fumbling with the buttons when it happened.

A critter jumped up from behind the parcel of hay. With a growl, it bit Steven's hand.

"Aah!" he cried, pulling back his bloody hand. Two fingers were missing. "My fingers! Something bit me!"

April gasped. What was going on? A moment later, she felt something move behind her. She scrambled away from it.

Straw flew through the air as a furry critter rolled out of the hay. It moved across the loft, then dove at Steven.

"Look out!" April screamed as the critter knocked Steven down. Then it buried its sharp teeth in his stomach. "No!" cried April. Steven was bleeding from his mouth and nose. The animal was killing him!

April grabbed the pitchfork and ran across the loft. Then she jabbed the critter with the sharp prongs.

The beast stopped eating and looked up at her. Its teeth glittered as it growled.

A critter attacks Steven.

April poked it again. This time, the critter just opened its mouth and bit off the end of the pitchfork. April screamed as it gobbled up the steel prongs. Its red eyes glowed. Then it came after her.

April screeched and beat at the critter with the broken pitchfork handle. But the monster would not back off. April was near the edge of the loft when she heard her brother's voice.

"April! Is that you?" Brad shouted from the barn door. He scurried up to the loft. When he reached the top of the ladder, he froze. He couldn't believe what he was seeing.

A small, furry monster stood in the center of the loft. It was only about a foot tall. But it had a huge mouth with rows of sharp teeth.

"This thing killed Steven," April shouted. She kept hitting it with the stick.

A normal coyote or barn rat would have run away. But this critter didn't seem scared at all. What could Brad do to save his sister?

Firepower.

Brad remembered the firecrackers he had stuffed into his pockets. He pulled out a small one and lit it.

"Help me!" April screamed. The critter was creeping toward her.

Brad tossed the firecracker at the monster. The critter picked it up and popped it in its mouth. With a smile, the critter swallowed it whole!

But a moment later, the monster began to tremble. Its eyes bugged out and its cheeks puffed up.

"It's exploding inside him!" Brad said.

A puff of smoke came out of the critter's mouth. Then the monster fell over.

"It's dead," said Brad.

18 "Let's get out of here!" April and Brad raced out of the barn.

"Get back to the house," yelled Brad. Dust flew as they ran. Brad slowed down to look back, and his heart pounded. The critters were chasing them! They rolled close behind them, nipping at their heels.

At last, they reached the front porch. Brad's mother stood at the door with a shotgun.

"Stay away from my family!" Helen Brown cried. Then she lifted the shotgun. She pulled the trigger, and a critter exploded.

Before the critters could attack again, the Browns scrambled into the house. Brad slammed the front door and threw the bolt. They had made it inside. But Brad knew they still weren't safe.

THE BOWL-A-RAMA

The bounty hunters cruised down the main street of town. They were driving Jeff's patrol car. And one of the hunters now looked like Jeff. He had transformed himself when they'd discovered Jeff's body.

"Stop here," ordered Johnny Steel. He wanted to ask the townspeople if they'd seen the crites.

They stopped in front of a one-story building. It had a sign with flashing lights that said BOWL-A-RAMA.

The hunters climbed out of the car and went inside.

The bowling alley was crowded. Everyone in town had come to watch the big contest.

Jay Brown's teammates stood beside a pay phone. They were upset that he was missing. "There's no answer," said the man holding the phone.

"I wonder what happened to Jay?" said another man.

Across the bowling alley, Charlie, the Browns' farmhand, was giving a speech. "They're here!" he shouted "The Martians are here! I can tell. They're giving me messages through my fillings." **19**

He pointed to his teeth.

The people ignored Charlie. They had heard his crazy stories before. But they couldn't ignore the hunters. Dressed in studded leather, they stood out in the crowd. Especially the hunter that looked like Jeff.

"Deputy?" asked one man. "Deputy Jeff, what's wrong with you?"

The hunter turned to the man. "Where are the crites?" he asked.

The man was confused. "What are you talking about?"

Johnny Steel lifted the man by his collar. "We want the crites," Steel said.

Johnny Steel asks about the crites.

"Crites?" said the man. "Who are they—some new bowling team?"

Steel dropped the man. These earthlings were not very helpful. He noticed a short, thin man edging closer. It was Charlie.

"Here they are—the aliens!" Charlie shouted. He pointed at the hunters. "I told you they were coming."

Suddenly, the hunter who looked like Jeff began to shake. There was a crackling noise. The hunter's face began to change shape. He was transforming again. Now he looked like Charlie.

"You—he—" Charlie was so scared, he didn't know what to say. "I'm getting out of here!" he screamed. He ran out of the bowling alley.

The hunter who looked like Charlie shrugged. These earth people were hard to understand. "Let's go."

Steel nodded. But before he left, he wanted to bowl. The earth sport looked like fun. Steel lifted a ball and tossed it down the lane. The ball zoomed through the air like a rocket. Then it hit the pins. They shattered into a white powder.

"Wow!" said one bowler.

"Hey, that's a strike," said another man.

But the bounty hunters were already gone.

TRAPPED INSIDE!

Inside the farmhouse, Brad and his sister sat by the fireplace. The family had tried to get away, but the critters had destroyed their truck. Now they were locked inside. They had boarded up the windows and doors. But Brad knew the critters would try to break in. Jay Brown was resting on the couch. His wife sat beside him.

"I wonder what those critters are?" said April.

"They're from outer space, like Charlie says," Brad answered. **21**

"Oh, Bradley." His mother sighed.

"Maybe they're some government test that went haywire," said Brad. "Like gophers that got zapped by gamma rays."

This time, Brad's parents didn't answer. He could see that they were tired and scared.

Suddenly, Brad heard a noise above him. It came from the chimney. A critter was trying to get in through the fireplace!

Brad and April spun around. They reached up and closed the flue—just in time.

"I think we stopped it," Brad said.

A moment later, another critter crashed through the window and sailed into the room. It landed on top of the couch. "Grrr!" it growled.

Brad's mother jumped off the couch and backed away. But she wasn't fast enough. The critter lowered its head and shot a dart at her. She fell to the floor.

Brad's mother is hit by a dart.

A critter sneaks up on Brad.

Now they'd hurt his mother! Brad kneeled down beside her. The poison dart was stuck in her neck. Brad pulled the dart out and helped her up.

April pushed the couch over. That stalled the monster for a minute and gave the Browns time to climb the stairs.

Jay Brown helped his wife into their bedroom. April was right behind them. When she reached the door, she saw a critter creeping up on Brad.

"Look out!" she cried.

Brad spun around. The critter growled and smiled up at him. It had cornered Brad.

Brad sets the hall rug on fire.

An oil lamp sat on the hall table. Brad grabbed it and threw it down. As it shattered, the flame spread to the hall rug. Suddenly, the critter was on fire!

"Yee!" the critter squealed. It ran around in circles. Then it rolled into the bathroom and jumped into the toilet.

Brad and April could hear a hissing noise as the critter doused itself. They stamped out the fire in the hall. Then they went into their parents' room.

Brad locked the door behind him. His family wasn't doing well. Their faces were pale. Their clothes were torn and bloody. They couldn't fight the critters much longer.

Brad gritted his teeth. "Dad," he said, "someone has to go for help."

Jay Brown nodded. "I've got to get to a phone. Get the sheriff out here . . ." he muttered.

"You can't even walk," Brad said. "Let me go."

"No way," his father said.

"I can do it, Dad," Brad insisted.

"Son," Jay Brown said after a moment, "if I said okay, what would you do?"

Brad squatted next to his father. "I'd hit the yard and head for the road. Dad, I'm the fastest thing we've got. Let me give it a try. Please?"

Jay Brown closed his eyes for a second. Then he looked up and grabbed Brad's arm. "Okay," he said. "But I want you to run like you never ran before."

Brad stood up. "Okay. Don't worry, Dad."

The fastest way out was through the window and down the tree. "After I leave, push this dresser in front of the window," Brad told April. "It'll help keep the critters out."

For once, April didn't look at Brad as if he were a pest. She jumped up to say good-bye. "Be careful," she told him. **25**

THE KILLER CLAW

As soon as Brad climbed out, April pushed the dresser in front of the window. She hoped Brad would get away from the critters outside. April couldn't stand to think of what would happen to her little brother in the jaws of those monsters.

Suddenly, the window behind her was smashed open. Glass flew over April's head.

"Look out!" said her father. "It's a huge critter. And he's trying to get in."

With all her might, April leaned back against the dresser. It rocked and swayed as the critter tried to push its way into the house. But April didn't give up.

A drawer flew out of the dresser and shot across the room. Then a huge, clawed hand snaked out from the hole.

April screamed as the critter's hand grabbed her arm. The claw pulled, trying to drag her away.

April wrestles with a giant claw.

"Help me!" she cried.

Her father hobbled to his feet. He raised the shotgun and fired.

The critter squealed and pulled back its claw. But the Browns knew the monsters would attack again. April could hear them through the walls. They were ripping apart the house, tearing up everything.

"Please, please hurry, Brad," April whispered.

ELP!

Brad was out of breath. He had run all the way to the highway, but not a single car had passed. Now he saw two headlights up ahead. He ran to the center of the road.

"Stop!" he called. He stood on the yellow line and waved his arms.

The car screeched to a stop. Brad was happy to see that it was a police car. He opened the door and jumped into the backseat.

"Let's go!" he said, pounding on the seat. "Those things—those critters have taken over our farm."

"Where are they?" asked the driver.

That didn't sound like Jeff. "Charlie?" Brad leaned forward to find Charlie behind the wheel. "Where's Deputy Jeff?" Brad asked.

Brad was confused. Why was Charlie dressed in that weird leather gear? The other guy was wearing it too. Brad studied the other man's face. It was that famous rock star. "Hey, you're Johnny Steel!" he said.

Steel turned around and grabbed Brad by the shirt. "We want the crites," he said.

"Crites?" Brad asked.

"Critters—crites," said the other hunter.

"Oh . . . they're at my house," said Brad.

"Where is that?" asked the driver.

Suddenly Brad realized that these guys weren't from Kansas. They were a little strange, but right now he could use all the help he could get.

"Okay," Brad said. "You help me and I'll help you. Drive straight ahead."

F IGHTING BACK

By the time Brad and the hunters arrived, the farmhouse was a mess. The windows were broken. The furniture had been ripped. Its stuffing covered the floor like puffy snowflakes.

"Mom? Dad?" Brad called from the hallway.

Upstairs, the bedroom door flew open. Brad's family came running down the stairs.

"Brad! Thank God you're safe," said his mother. She hugged him.

Brad introduced the bounty hunters. "These guys are looking for the critters," he explained.

The Browns were happy for the help, though Brad's father seemed confused. "That guy looks a lot like Charlie," he said.

Outside a siren wailed.

"The sheriff's here!" April said thankfully.

"Let's get out of here," said Jay Brown. He guided his wife outside. "Come on, son."

Brad was about to follow when he heard a meow from upstairs. "Chewy?" he called. The cat meowed again.

The hunters' boots pounded as they climbed the stairs. Brad was right behind them.

Upstairs, Brad showed Johnny Steel where the critter had jumped into the toilet. When Steel lifted the lid, the critter squealed. It was still alive!

The hunters fight back.

Steel fired his laser gun. The whole house rocked, and the toilet exploded.

"Wow!" said Brad. All that was left of the critter was a torn piece of fur.

Steel turned to Brad. "Thanks for the tip, kid."

While the hunters searched the house, Brad found Chewy in his bedroom. He had just picked up the cat when he heard a scream outside.

K IDNAPPED!

"April's gone!" Brad's mother cried. She was sobbing.

Brad raced outside. Sheriff Harve stood in the driveway. He seemed embarrassed. "I tried to stop them," he said, "but they move so fast."

"They dragged her off to the back field," said Brad's father.

April had been kidnapped! Brad was too mad to speak. He just jumped on his bike and pedaled. He didn't even stop when his parents called him.

It was still dark. But Brad could see a track in the weeds where they had dragged April. He followed it for a mile or so, until it led to an open field. In the center of the field sat a round spaceship. Its door was open—and the critters were dragging April inside.

"It's a flying saucer!" Brad said aloud.

"It sure is!" a voice answered. Charlie stepped out from behind a tree.

"Charlie," Brad said. "What are you doing here?"

Charlie pointed to his mouth. "I just followed my fillings. I've been getting signals like crazy."

"The critters got April," Brad explained. "I have to save her." He began to sneak closer to the ship.

"Get back here, boy!" Charlie said. "Or they'll get you too!" **31**

But Brad didn't listen. He had to save his sister. He climbed to the mouth of the ship. He could see the critters inside, huddled in one corner. April was asleep on the floor.

Moving silently, Brad went to her. He pulled a poison dart from her neck.

April stirred. "Where am I?"

"Shh!" Brad helped her up. "We've got to get out of here."

Brad and April started to scramble out of the ship. They had almost made it to the door when April slipped. Brad caught her, but the noise gave them away. The critters cackled and started after them.

At last, April jumped out to freedom. Brad paused at the door and reached into his pocket. He pulled out a firecracker—the biggest explosive he had ever made. He wanted the critters to leave with a bang. But when he tried to light it, the ship began to rock. Brad fell out of the ship. The firecracker landed inside.

"They're taking off!" April shouted. She helped Brad to his feet. "Let's go—before they come back for dessert!"

"Come on, you two!" Charlie shouted.

"No—wait. I dropped my firecracker in the ship," Brad explained. "But it wasn't lit."

Charlie stopped running. "One of your homemade specials is inside that ship?" he asked.

Brad nodded.

"We've got to get it lit!" Charlie pulled a lighter from his shirt pocket. "Do you have any more firecrackers?" he asked Brad.

Brad searched his pockets. "No. That was my last one."

"Well, then," said Charlie, "this'll have to do." Charlie threw the flaming lighter at the spaceship.

Although the ship was taking off, the door was just sliding closed. Charlie's lighter soared through the air and landed just

inside the doorway.

The ground trembled as the critters' ship lifted off and climbed into the sky.

Brad was watching the ship when he heard a car behind him in the field. It was Sheriff Harve's patrol car. Brad's parents were in the back, and the two hunters rode in front beside Harve.

"Mom, Dad," April said, "Brad saved me from the critters."

Helen and Jay Brown rushed over to their children.

"Thank goodness you're both all right!" said Brad's mother.

The critters' ship flew overhead. It looped through the sky. Then it dipped low over the Browns' farmhouse on the hill. Suddenly a bolt of light shot out from the ship. Then there was a huge explosion on the ground. The critters had bombed the house! A huge fireball lit the horizon. Everyone watched as the flames swallowed the farmhouse.

The Browns watch in horror as their house bursts into flames.

"That's our home!" sobbed Helen Brown.

Inside the ship, the critters laughed. They loved getting revenge. When their laughter died down, they heard a noise on the ship. It was a sizzling sound.

One critter noticed Brad's firecracker. The fuse had caught fire. "Uh-oh!" said the critter.

Another explosion lit the sky. The critters' ship was blown up into tiny pieces.

"Wow!" Brad shouted. "My firecracker worked!"

"Mission complete," said Johnny Steel.

The space hunters began to walk back to their ship. But Brad ran after them.

"Hey, wait!" he called.

The hunters paused.

"I just wanted to say thanks," Brad said.

Steel nodded. He waved his hand over his belt buckle, and it started to glow. A piece came off in his hand. He gave it to Brad. "Call me," said Steel.

"Thanks," Brad said. The gizmo from Steel's belt glowed in his hand. It looked like some kind of signaling device.

The hunters strode away. Everyone else piled into the sheriff's car.

N O PLACE LIKE HOME

The sun was coming up. Harve drove them back to the ruined farm.

The critters had destroyed everything. Piles of smoking ashes covered the ground where the house used to be. The sight made Brad sick.

Suddenly Brad heard a beeping sound. It was coming from the gizmo Steel had given him. He took the small box out of his pocket and saw that a button was flashing. Not sure what to do, Brad pressed the button.

A fierce wind began to howl. It swept around the Browns but began to scatter the piles of rubble. Wooden planks were lifted into the air. Pieces of glass jingled into place.

"Is it a twister?" April asked.

"No—look!" Brad pointed to where the house used to be. The wind was stacking boards and shingles in place. Their home was being put back together! Shiny glass windows were tucked in place. A solid roof was clamped on top. The last piece to go in place was the mailbox.

When it was finished, the Browns were amazed. Brad's parents hugged each other.

A muffled meow caught Brad's ear. "Chewy?" he said. He found the family cat in the mailbox. Chewy jumped into his arms and gave a loud meow.

A moment later, April pointed at the sky. "Look!"

A spaceship soared overhead. It dipped low over the valley, as if to say good-bye.

"It's the hunters," Brad said, waving. He was grateful for their help.

The Brown family was safe again. Cows grazed in the pasture. Birds sang in the trees. The smell of bacon came from the kitchen. Mrs. Brown was making breakfast.

Inside the chicken coop, three eggs wiggled around. They didn't look like chicken eggs. They were shaped like pinecones. And they made an eerie, cackling sound, like laughter.

The critter eggs cackled again. They couldn't wait to hatch!

Are the critters gone forever?

BEHIND THE SCENES

Those bloodthirsty monsters in *Critters* were scary—especially when their sharp teeth were gnawing on a victim! But one of the most frightening things about the critters was that they came from the unknown—outer space. Scientists don't know for sure whether life exists in outer space. What amazing—or horrible—creatures could soar through the universe and land on earth?

For centuries people have wondered if life exists among the stars and planets. Countless sightings of flying saucers and strange airships have been recorded.

One legend claims that people in Ireland saw a spaceship back in the 1200s! Villagers were gathered in church when they heard a noise on the roof. They ran outside and found an anchor stuck in the church roof. The anchor hung from a long rope. When the people looked up, they saw that the rope was dangling from a ship that floated in the sky!

A more recent sighting took place in Roswell, New Mexico, in

1947. The local papers reported people seeing odd lights in the sky. And a flying disk actually landed on a ranch near Roswell! The U.S. Army rushed out to the ranch and picked up the disk. They took it back to their base to study it. The army reported that the disk was a weather balloon that had crashed to the ground. But many people believe the disk was part of a flying saucer from outer space.

Hollywood has produced its share of movies about flying saucers and the invasion of alien creatures. *Critters* is special because the hero of the story is a 12-year-old. If it weren't for Brad Brown, critters might have gobbled up the state of Kansas! And Brad receives help from a surprising source—outer space. The bounty hunters are aliens, even if they are friendly guys who can dress like rock stars. The writers of *Critters* show us that there might be both good and evil creatures lurking in outer space.

F LOATING IN SPACE?

The strangest-looking creature in the film was Warden Zanti, the keeper of the asteroid prison. His odd-shaped head was actually a hat made of foam latex. This sponge-like headpiece was glued onto the actor's head. Then heavy white makeup was applied to the actor's face. The makeup made the headpiece blend into the actor's skin so that it seemed to be part of Zanti's head.

But it takes time to create a space alien. It took three hours to complete Zanti's makeup!

Zanti's round body had no legs or feet. He was perched in a small flying saucer that hovered in the air. This special effect was done with the help of a crane. Zanti's saucer was actually a bucket attached to a small crane kept out of camera range. The arm of the crane was hidden behind Zanti's body. As the crane's bucket moved back and forth, Zanti seemed to be floating in midair.

The actor who plays the bounty hunter on the right can't see a thing under his mask!

MEN WITHOUT FACES

The makeup for the bounty hunters was very simple. Before they "transformed," their faces were smooth, white masks. To achieve this look, the actors wore white plastic hoods, similar to bathing caps. The hoods were easy to put on. But they gave the actors a few problems. They couldn't breathe or see through them!

Each actor had to breathe through a hose placed in his mouth. The hose ran under the mask into the actor's clothes. The other end of the hose stuck out of a hole in the actor's costume. **39**

If breathing was a problem, talking was out of the question. Though the hunters rarely spoke, in the scenes where they did, their voices had to be dubbed in later.

Since the hunters couldn't see through the plastic hoods, they had to rehearse each scene without their masks. They carefully counted their steps and took note of obstacles on the set. Despite their practice, there were a few times when the actors tripped and fell. It's not easy getting around on a movie set when you're blinded by a mask!

# **M** ELTDOWN

When the hunters transformed, their faces changed and contorted. Bone, muscle, teeth and skin seemed to form before our very eyes! It looked as if actor Terrence Mann was turning from a skeleton into a human being. In fact, Mann was not present while this scene was being filmed. This amazing scene was the brainchild of makeup artist Christopher Biggs. He created it with the help of time-lapse photography.

Chris started by making a life cast of Mann's face. He covered the actor's face with plaster. When the plaster dried, he pulled it off in one solid piece. That piece was used as a mold. It was filled with plaster to create a realistic, life-size dummy head.

Next Chris crafted several versions of the dummy head. He wanted to show the hunter's face forming from the skeleton up. So he made heads that showed different layers of the body. One head was just a bony skull. One head had facial muscles made of red gelatin. To get the muscles right, Chris consulted a book on human anatomy. One head had teeth and eyes. Another head looked nearly human, covered with skin.

In the studio, each head was filmed separately. Chris built a reusable dummy of the shoulders and chest. A dummy head was attached to the shoulders. Then the melting began.

Two propane heaters were fired up and pointed at the head. The heaters were as loud as jet rockets. Their heat turned the gelatin to liquid. The goop oozed, then ran off the edges of the head as it melted away. This process was repeated with each head. In the end, they had shots of more than half a dozen heads with melting surfaces.

Although the hunter seemed to be sitting up, this scene was filmed at an angle. The dummy was lying flat. The camera filmed from overhead. This way, when the gelatin melted, it seemed to disappear. In fact, the goop dripped off-camera. Each head took about 30 minutes to melt. But it sometimes took longer to clean up the gelatin that had dripped all over the set!

The final touch for this effect came in the editing stage. When the film of each meltdown was reversed and speeded up, it looked as if the layers of bone, muscle and skin were forming! A few bone-crunching sound effects were added to make a scene you'll never forget.

B UILDING A CRITTER

The grisly critters were designed and operated by three brothers: Steve, Charlie and Ed Chiodo. How is a critter made? The Chiodos started off with a fiberglass skull. They covered that with foam-rubber skin and stiff, spiky hair that actually came from moose pelts!

The critters' clawlike arms also were made of foam rubber. After the arms were painted, hard acrylic nails were glued to their claws. You might say that each critter got a personal manicure.

The critters had cold red eyes that seemed to light up. In fact, electricity had nothing to do with this creepy effect. The critters' eyes were clear Plexiglas balls, like glass marbles. The back of each **41**

Moose hair is glued to a critter's skin.

ball was painted with red reflective paint. This type of paint is used on some stop signs. Have you ever noticed how street signs seem to light up when headlights hit them at night? That's because reflective paint makes the light bounce back. When light hit the critters' eyes, the red paint made the light bounce, and the eyes seemed to burn like red bulbs.

The critter arms drying—what a mess!

The Chiodo brothers had to build more than a dozen critter models for the film. Although the critters are the size of softballs when curled up, they grow when they eat. The filmmakers needed 12-inch monsters, as well as one 4-foot critter suit to be worn by a dwarf at the end of the movie.

Here's the actor who plays the human-size critter.

The critter crew—how many critter models can you find in this picture?

J UMPING CRITTERS

Most of the critters were hand puppets. During much of the movie the critters were operated by Steve Chiodo's hand. Remember the scene in the hayloft when the critter jumped up and bit off Steven's fingers? Steve Chiodo was hiding behind the haystack, working the puppet. The actor playing Steven folded his fingers down so that fake fingers could be glued to his knuckles. Chiodo's puppet simply hopped up and ripped the false fingers off with its rubber teeth.

The critter's leap into the toilet was another simple stunt. A crew member stood off-camera and tossed the critter into the bowl as if it were a basketball!

To operate the critters, the Chiodos used four techniques:

1. They pitched them as if they were bowling balls. This worked well in the outdoor scenes. It was easy to roll a bunch of furry balls down a hillside.

2. They pulled them with piano wire. This thin wire is nearly invisible to the camera lens.

3. They moved them with radio-controlled devices. If you've ever seen a model car or plane operated by remote control, you've seen this technique in action.

4. They operated them with cables. When you use the hand brakes on a bike, you use cables. This is how the Chiodos changed the expressions on the critters' faces. Remember how the critter's face puffed up after it swallowed a firecracker? That effect was done with cables.

B LOWING UP THE SET

Critters was filmed in Newhall, California. The story takes place in Kansas. But the producers chose Newhall because it's close to their studio in Los Angeles and because the town's open fields resemble a midwestern farm.

Before shooting began, the crew built the entire set from scratch. The barn and cozy farmhouse were perfect, except for one thing. Each building was missing an entire wall. The three-sided set gave the camera operators and lighting crew room to do their jobs.

Filming ended with a bang. Demolition experts came to Newhall to blow up the set. The ball of fire and flying debris that you see in the movie is a real explosion.

The explosion that ended the filming—and destroyed the set!

Eight months after filming was finished, the filmmakers wanted to change the movie. They thought the ending—the Browns were left without a home—was too downbeat.

Someone came up with the idea of the bounty hunters putting the farm back together. The filmmakers loved it. There was only one problem. The farm was gone.

SPECIAL EFFECTS TO THE RESCUE

The studio hired a special-effects team called Fantasy II to build a miniature of the house. The team had to match every detail of the farmhouse, from the white picket fence to the number and shape of the windows. When the miniature house was completed, the crew moved it from the studio to Newhall, where the original house had been.

The new house was only 6 feet tall and 16 feet wide! Because of its small size, the crew had to place it on a platform and point special lights at it. The minihouse was also placed much closer to the actors. In this way, the filmmakers created the illusion that the house was larger and farther away.

The actors were called back to the set. On the first day, "reaction" shots were filmed—the camera recorded the Browns looking happily at their rebuilt house.

On the second day, the crew started to pull the house apart. While the cameras rolled, the miniature house began to crumble. This was done by pulling cables attached to the frame of the house. When reversed, this film made the house look as if it were leaping up out of the ground and rebuilding itself.

Thanks to the magic of special effects, the Browns got their farm back—at least until those eggs hatch!